Where's my share?

for
John, Helena,
Thomas, Patrick
and James

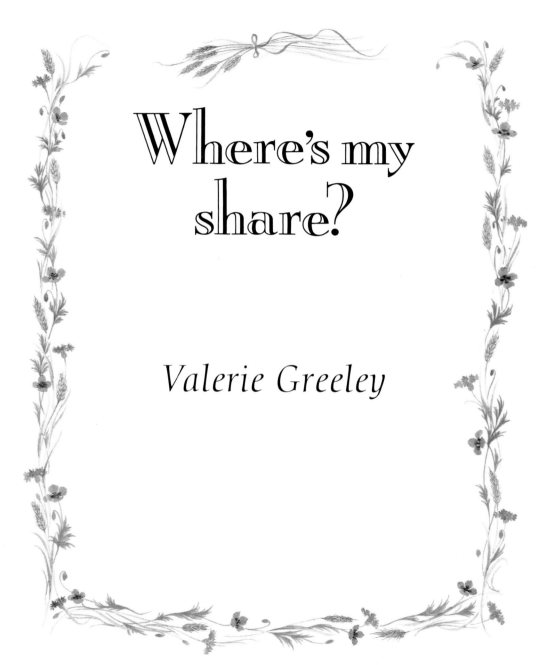

Where's my share?

Valerie Greeley

Blackie

What's in there?

A loaf of bread.

Where's my share?

A mouse took it.

Where is the mouse?

In her house.

Where is her house?

In the wood.

Where is the wood?

Covered in snow.

Where is the snow?

The sun melted it.

Where is the sun?

Ripening the corn.

Where is the corn?

Milled into flour.

Where is the flour?

Baked into bread.

Where's my share?

The inspiration for this story was
the rhyme 'What's in there?'
from *The Oxford Nursery Rhyme Book*
by Iona and Peter Opie.

Copyright © 1989 Valerie Greeley

First published in 1989 by
Blackie and Son Limited
7 Leicester Place, London WC2H 7BP

British Library Cataloguing in Publication Data
Greeley, Valerie
Where's my share?
1. English language. Readers – For pre-school
children
I. Title
428.6
ISBN 0-216-92748-X

Typeset in Diotima by Jigsaw Graphics, London

Printed in Hong Kong